DIRTY BERTIE

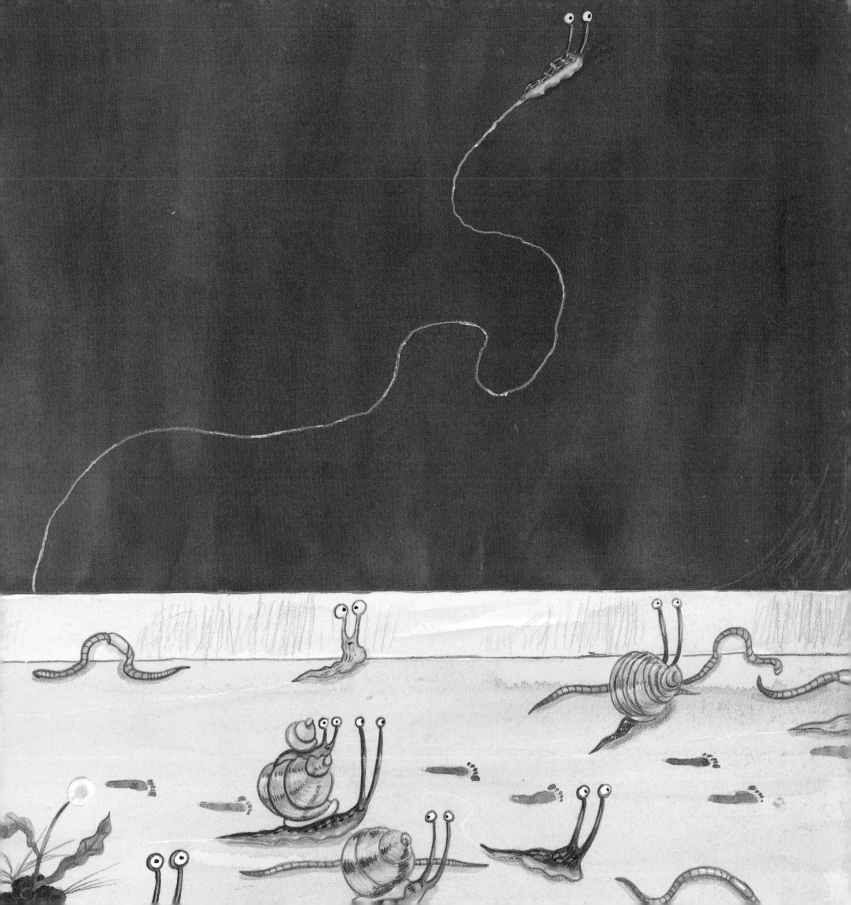

for Julia

KOALA BOOKS
www.koalabooks.com.au
First Australian edition published in 2002
by Koala Books, 4 Merchant Street, Mascot,
NSW, 2020, Australia

First published in Great Britain 2002
by LITTLE TIGER PRESS
1 The Coda Centre, 189 Munster Road, London SW6 6AW

2 4 6 8 10 9 7 5 3 1

© David Roberts 2002

Printed in Belgium by Proost

ISBN 0 86461 443 8

DIRTY BERTIE

David Roberts

Koala Books
www.koalabooks.com.au

This is Bertie.
He used to have dirty habits.

If Bertie saw a sweet on the floor,
he would pick it up and eat it.

But Bertie's mum would shout ...

"NO, BERTIE! THAT'S DIRTY, BERTIE!"

If Bertie had a bogey up his nose, he'd try to pick it out.

But Bertie's dad would shout ...

"NO, BERTIE! THAT'S DIRTY, BERTIE!"

Bertie liked to go hunting for
slugs and worms in the garden,
and play with them.

But Bertie's big sister, Suzy, would shout …

"NO, BERTIE! THAT'S DIRTY, BERTIE!"

Sometimes, Bertie's dog would lick his face,
so Bertie would lick him back.

But Bertie's gran would shout ...

"NO, BERTIE! THAT'S DIRTY, BERTIE!"

If Bertie saw his cat do a wee on the flowerbed,
Bertie would do a wee on the flowerbed too.

But everyone would shout ...

"NO, BERTIE! THAT'S DIRTY, BERTIE!"

Bertie soon learned not to …

wee in the flowerbed ...

or play with slugs and worms ...

or eat sweets off the floor ...

or even lick the dog's face.

bleugh!

But there is one dirty habit that
Bertie cannot stop!

When no one is looking,
he still picks bogeys
out of his nose ...

and sometimes...

he eats them!

UGH!